Dear Parent:

Congratulations! Your child is taking the first steps on an exciting journey. The destination? Independent reading!

STEP INTO READING® will help your child get there. The program offers five steps to reading success. Each step includes fun stories and colorful art. There are also Step into Reading Sticker Books, Step into Reading Math Readers, Step into Reading Phonics Readers, Step into Reading Write-In Readers, and Step into Reading Phonics Boxed Sets—a complete literacy program with something to interest every child.

Learning to Read, Step by Step!

Ready to Read   **Preschool–Kindergarten**
• big type and easy words • rhyme and rhythm • picture clues
For children who know the alphabet and are eager to begin reading.

Reading with Help   **Preschool–Grade 1**
• basic vocabulary • short sentences • simple stories
For children who recognize familiar words and sound out new words with help.

Reading on Your Own   **Grades 1–3**
• engaging characters • easy-to-follow plots • popular topics
For children who are ready to read on their own.

Reading Paragraphs   **Grades 2–3**
• challenging vocabulary • short paragraphs • exciting stories
For newly independent readers who read simple sentences with confidence.

Ready for Chapters   **Grades 2–4**
• chapters • longer paragraphs • full-color art
For children who want to take the plunge into chapter books but still like colorful pictures.

STEP INTO READING® is designed to give every child a successful reading experience. The grade levels are only guides. Children can progress through the steps at their own speed, developing confidence in their reading, no matter what their grade.

Remember, a lifetime love of reading starts with a single step!

For Emma —R.H.

Step into Reading, Random House, and the Random House colophon are registered trademarks of Random House, Inc.

Visit us on the Web!
StepIntoReading.com
randomhouse.com/kids

Educators and librarians, for a variety of teaching tools, visit us at
randomhouse.com/teachers

ISBN 978-0-7364-2908-5 (trade) — ISBN 978-0-7364-8106-9 (lib. bdg.)
Printed in the United States of America
10 9 8 7 6 5 4 3 2 1

STEP INTO READING®

Jewels for a Princess

By Ruth Homberg
Illustrated by Studio IBOIX, Andrea Cagol,
Gabriella Matta, Cristina Spagnoli, Valeria Turati,
and the Disney Storybook Artists

Random House 🏠 New York

The Prince
gives Cinderella
a sparkly blue ring.
She loves it!

Cinderella shows
her new ring
to her friends.

Gus wants a ring,
too.
He finds
something shiny.
It is just a marble.

Cinderella shares
her ring with Gus.
He puts it
on his tail!

Cinderella loves
her friends.
They are
the best gift!

Jasmine finds
a fancy jewel.
Whose is it?

A guard gives Jasmine
the purple jewel.
It is a surprise
from Aladdin!

Jasmine puts the jewel
in her hair.
It sparkles and shines.

Aladdin and Abu
take Jasmine
on a magic carpet ride.
She loves
her new jewel.

Jasmine loves
Aladdin and Abu
most of all.

Aurora gets
a new crown.
It has a lovely
pink jewel.

Aurora is
a pretty princess!
A painter paints
her picture.

The Good Fairies
wave their wands.
The jewel shines!

Aurora thanks
her family and friends
for the crown.
She is so happy!

Ariel swims and plays
with her friends.

They find
many jewels.
Flounder shares them
with Ariel.

King Triton
makes a jewel necklace.
He puts the necklace
around Ariel's neck.

The jewel
reminds Ariel
of her friends
in the sea.

Rapunzel wears

a tiara that glitters.

It has red, white,
and green jewels.

Flynn thinks Rapunzel
is a perfect princess!

Tiana and Naveen go
to the bayou.
Naveen gives Tiana
a special stone.

Tiana thanks Naveen.
She gives him
a big hug.

Mama Odie makes

the stone shimmer.

It is

the perfect gift.

Tiana loves
her new jewel.
She wears it
to a party.

She thanks Mama Odie
and Naveen.

Tiana's friends are
the best jewels of all!

No Boredom Allowed!

PAPER
GAMES &
PENCIL
PUZZLES

written by FLORENCE QUINN

illustrated by ETHAN LONG

STERLING

New York / London

www.sterlingpublishing.com/kids

STERLING and the distinctive Sterling logo are registered trademarks of
Sterling Publishing Co., Inc.

2 4 6 8 10 9 7 5 3 1
03/09
Published by Sterling Publishing Co., Inc.
387 Park Avenue South, New York, NY 10016
Text © 2009 by Sterling Publishing Co., Inc
Illustrations © 2009 by Ethan Long
Distributed in Canada by Sterling Publishing
C/o Canadian Manda Group, 165 Dufferin Street
Toronto, Ontario, Canada M6K 3H6
Distributed in the United Kingdom by GMC Distribution Services
Castle Place, 166 High Street, Lewes, East Sussex, England BN7 1XU
Distributed in Australia by Capricorn Link (Australia) Pty. Ltd.
P.O. Box 704, Windsor, NSW 2756, Australia

Printed in China
All rights reserved

Sterling ISBN 978-1-4027-5948-2

For information about custom editions, special sales, premium and
corporate purchases, please contact Sterling Special Sales
Department at 800-805-5489 or specialsales@sterlingpublishing.com.

CONTENTS

SHARPEN YOUR PENCIL AND YOUR BRAIN!

Welcome to a world of paper games and pencil puzzles, where no boredom is allowed and you can have fun for hours! The activities in this book are designed to keep you busy, spark some creativity, and provide hours of entertainment.

Part One is all about paper games. There are tons of pages for you to color in, cut out, wear, decorate, and play with. You will be constructing your own games out of paper. Some games you can play by yourself, and for some you'll need two or more players, so grab a sister, a brother, or a few friends.

The pencil puzzles in Part Two will fuel your brain and send you into a creative spin—and some might keep you guessing. There are doodles, mazes, dot-to-dots, and more cool pages with oodles of fun. You know you'll need a pencil for this—and make sure it's sharpened!

So, flip the page and get started. There's no time to waste when there's so much fun to be had . . . .

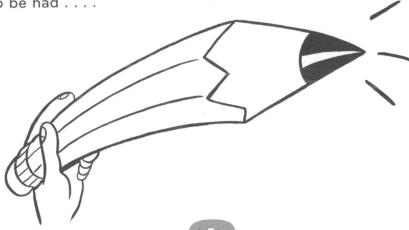

PART ONE

· ·

PAPER GAMES

FORTUNE TELLER

What you will need:

• scissors   • crayons   • pen or pencil

Directions:

1. Start by cutting out the square on page 9.

2. Fold corner 1 to touch corner 2. This should fold the square in half so it looks like a triangle.

3. Fold corner "RED" to touch corner "BLUE," forming a smaller triangle.

4. Open the paper up, unfolding all the folds you have just made.

5. Fold corners 1 and 2 in to the center point. Then fold corners 3 and 4 to the center. You should end up with a square.

6. Flip the square over. Fold one of the corners over to the center point. Fold over the remaining three corners to the center. You'll end up with a smaller square.

7. Fold the square in half. Unfold and fold in half the other way. Then, flip the square over and again fold it in half both ways.

8. Place your right thumb under the square that has "Blue" in the corner, and your right forefinger under the square that says "Green." Then place your left forefinger under the square that has "Red" in the corner, and your left thumb under the square that says "Orange." Push your fingers together so that the top corners of all the squares touch, making a diamond-like shape. You should be able to move these parts around.

9. Remove your fingers, and place the square—blank side up—on a flat surface. Write the numbers one through eight on the triangular flaps, one number per flap.

10. Write a fortune on the inside of each of the eight flaps underneath the numbers. Some examples of fortunes include:

YOU WILL HAVE A GOOD REPORT CARD THIS TERM

YOU WILL MAKE LOTS OF MONEY

GOOD FORTUNE WILL FOLLOW YOU WHEREVER YOU GO

SMILE AT SOMEONE TODAY

YOU WILL HAVE GOOD LUCK THIS WEEK

11. Decorate your fortune teller with crayons.

12. You can now be a fortune teller! Have a friend choose one of the four colors. Spell out the chosen color while moving the fortune teller in and out. Then have your friend choose one of the numbers that is showing on the inside. Move the fortune teller in and out that number of times. When you finish, have your friend choose another one of the four visible numbers. Open up the flap and read tell your friend's fortune.

1

3

4

2

GREEN

BLUE

RED

ORANGE

DOTS

What you will need:

- two or more players
- different colored pencils or pens for each player

Directions:

1. Players take turns drawing lines between dots on a grid. Each turn should produce one line in between two dots.
2. When a player completes a box, the player should initial the center of the box.
3. When the whole grid is filled with boxes, count up the number of boxes you've created. The player who completes the most boxes wins.

Dare Chooser

What you will need:

• safety scissors   • crayons   • pen or pencil   • glue   • drinking straw   • tape

Directions:

1. Cut out the template on the next page. Decorate and color your dare chooser before you begin folding and gluing. Invent four fun dares and write one in each of the four boxes. Sample dare: "Sing a song to the person sitting on your right."

2. Very carefully, cut the small circle in the box top. You can also use your pencil to carefully punch a hole in the paper.

3. Fold along all the solid lines.

4. Flatten the dare chooser, printed side up, and apply glue to the four tabs on the triangles and the tab on the side of the box. Carefully glue the bottom triangles to one another and then glue the side tab to the other side of the box.

5. Cut four small slits around the bottom of the drinking straw. Fold back these four tabs—they will keep the straw from sliding out of the box top. Push the straw through the hole from the inside out, and pull until the tabs are resting on the inside of the box top, then tape the tabs down. Cut off a few inches from the top of the straw.

6. Add glue to the rest of the tabs on the box, and seal up the top of the dare chooser.

7. You are now ready to spin . . . if you dare!

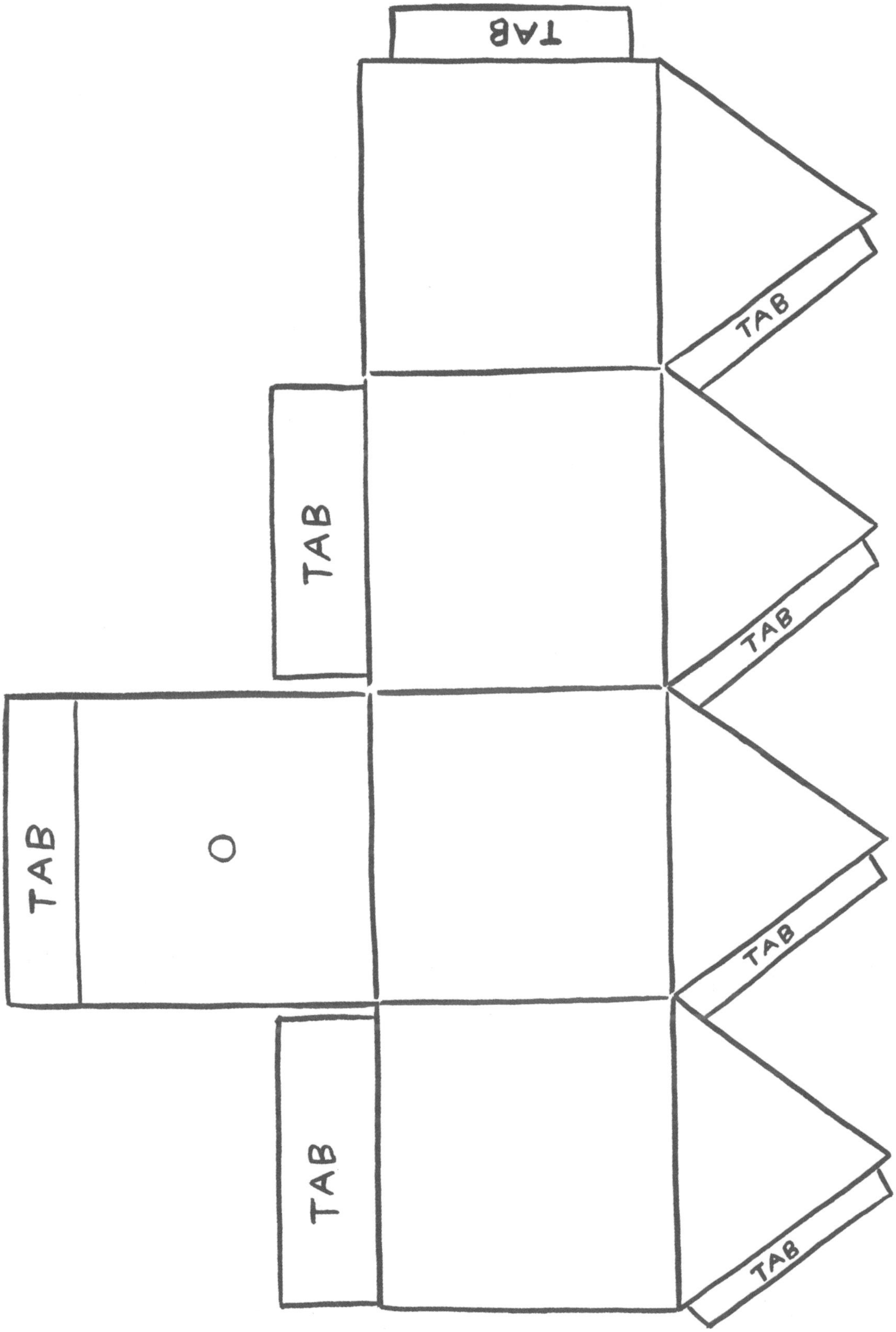

TAB

TAB

TAB

TAB

O

TAB

TAB

TAB

TAB

13

make your own masks

Color and decorate these masks. Once you've cut them out along all the solid lines, here's how to finish them and make them wearable: Staple an elastic string at either side near the ears and wear the mask around your head, or glue a wooden stick to the back of the mask on one side and hold the mask up to your face.

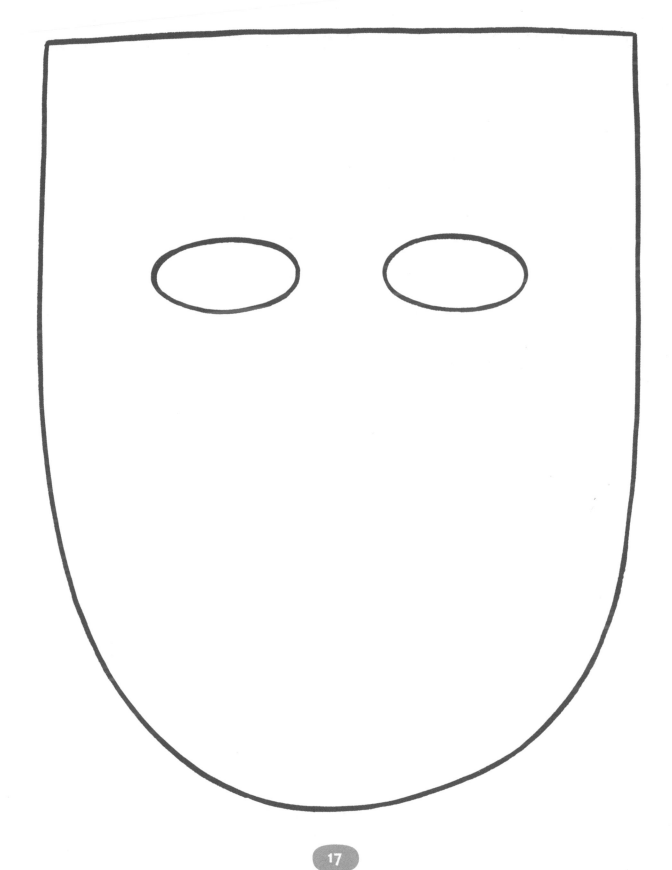

SPIRAL FUN

What you will need:

• crayons   • safety scissors   • string   • clothes hanger

Directions:

1. Color the spiral templates shown below and on page 23 and then cut the circles out carefully.
2. Cut along the spiraled lines inside the circles.
3. Punch a small hole in the top of each spiral where the x's are, and thread a string through each hole. Secure each spiral to its string by tying a knot.
4. Tie the other ends of the strings to a clothes hanger. Watch the spirals spin!

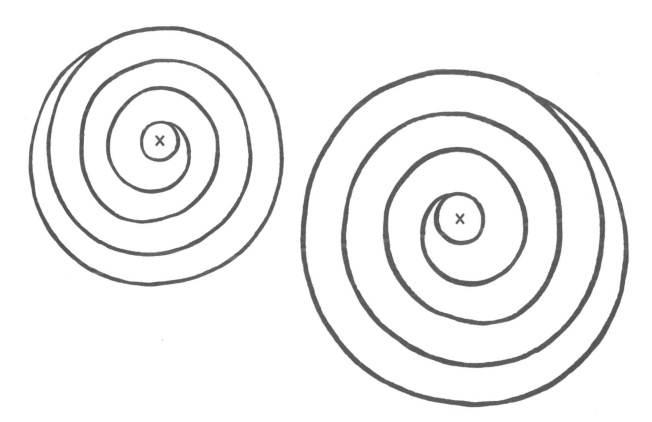

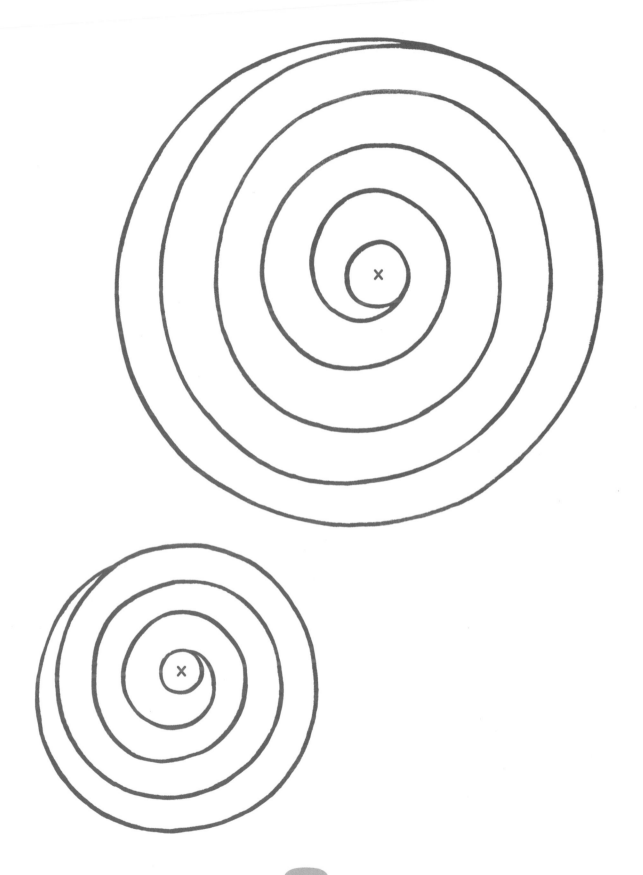

PaPeR FOOTBaLL

1. Cut out this rectangle along the solid lines.
2. Fold along the vertical dotted line in the center of the rectangle.
3. Fold along the second dotted line. You should now have a long, narrow piece of paper.
4. Beginning with the bottom right corner of the paper, fold up and toward the left edge of the paper to start forming a paper triangle.
5. Follow and fold along the dotted lines all the way up the page until you're left with a square tab at the top.
6. Tuck the square tab in to the top pocket of the triangle to secure it.
7. Now you have a paper football! You'll find directions how to play on page 27.

Tuck this tab into the top pocket of your triangle.

first fold →

second fold →

fold up

start folding the triangle from this corner

25

What you will need:

- safety scissors   • two players

Directions:

1. Cut up the template on page 25 and fold it along the dotted lines into a paper football. Spread out the football field, located on page 28.
2. Place the paper football in the palm of your hand and flick the football with your finger (from the other hand) to start the play. Wherever the football lands on the field is where the rest of the play will continue.
3. The object of the game is to score a touchdown, or goal. The edge of your paper, or "field," is your end zone. To score, you must flick the ball with your finger so it lands at least partially hanging over the edge of the field. If the ball goes farther than the field, it is out of bounds. A touchdown scores six points.
4. Players take turns back and forth. If the ball goes off the table, the other player gets to kick off and start the play again. If you score a touchdown, you get an extra kick to try and score one extra point.

To kick for an extra point:

- The opponent forms a goalpost by placing both elbows on the table, with arms up and thumbs touching. Extend index fingers to form the uprights.
- The kicker balances the football vertically between the index finger and the table. The kicker then flicks the football with his finger (from the other hand) to launch it in the air and through the goalpost. If the ball sails between the two goalposts, score an extra point.

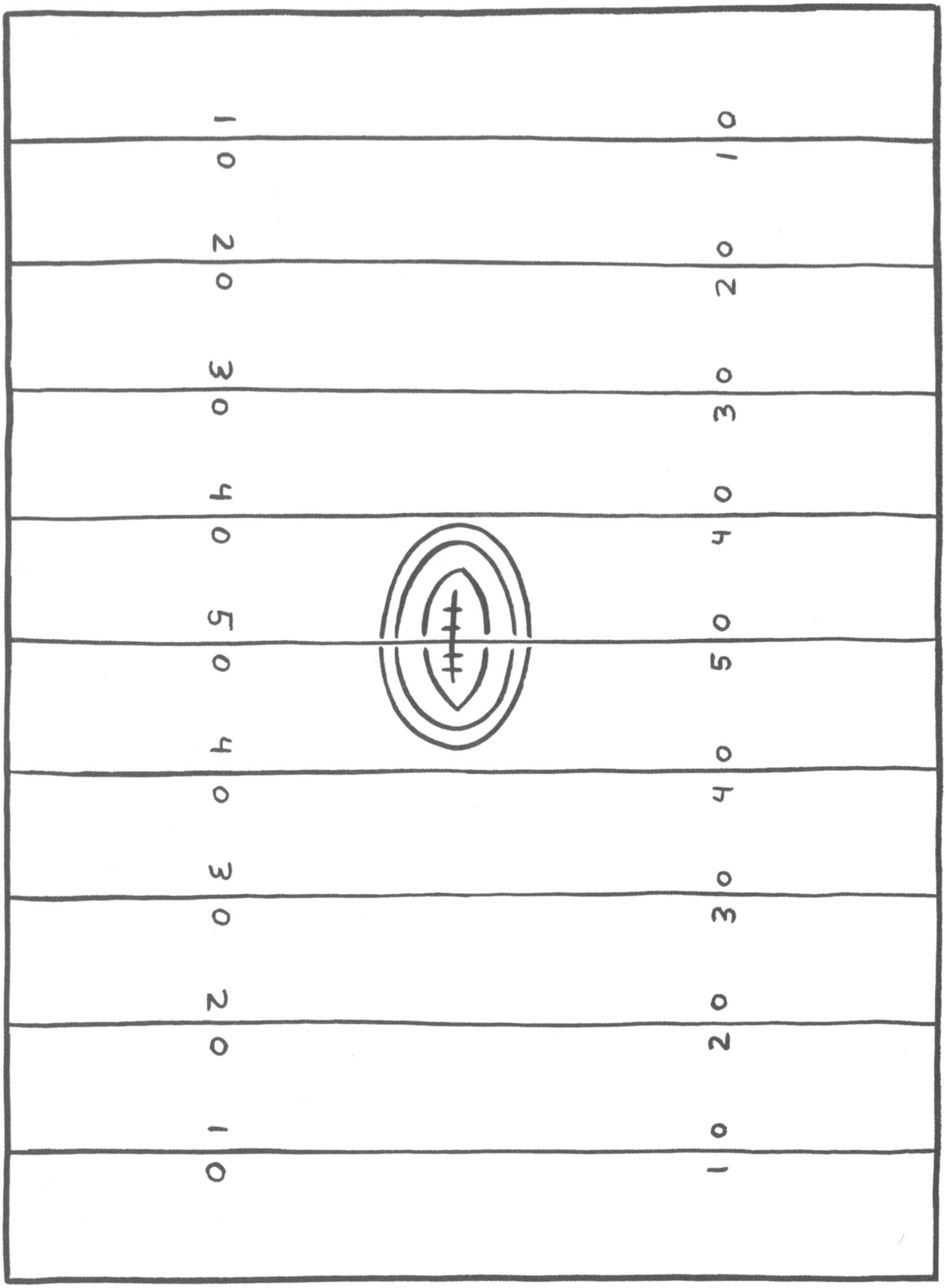
10 20 30 40 50 40 30 20 10
10 20 30 40 50 40 30 20 10

snowflakes

Fold along the dotted line, then cut along the edge of the design to make your own snowflakes!

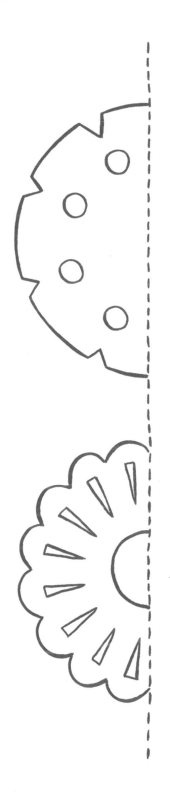

TIC-TAC-TOE

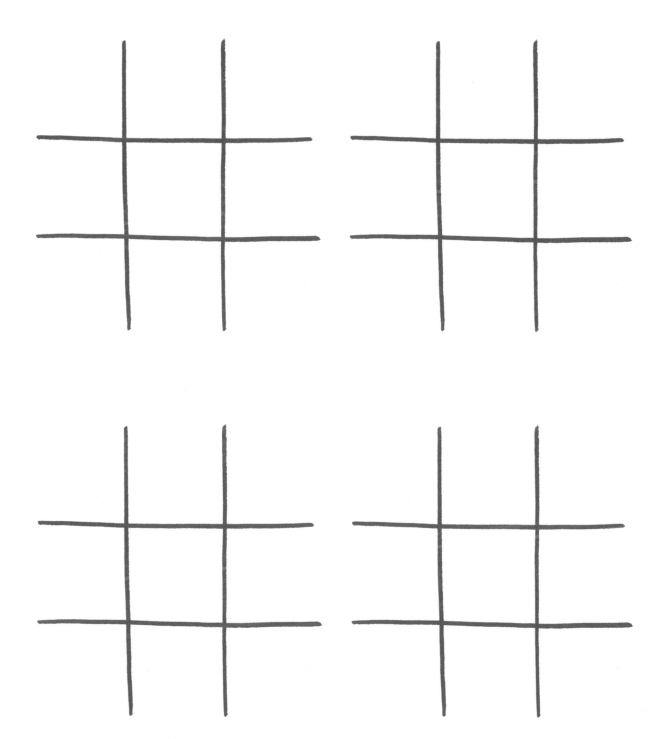

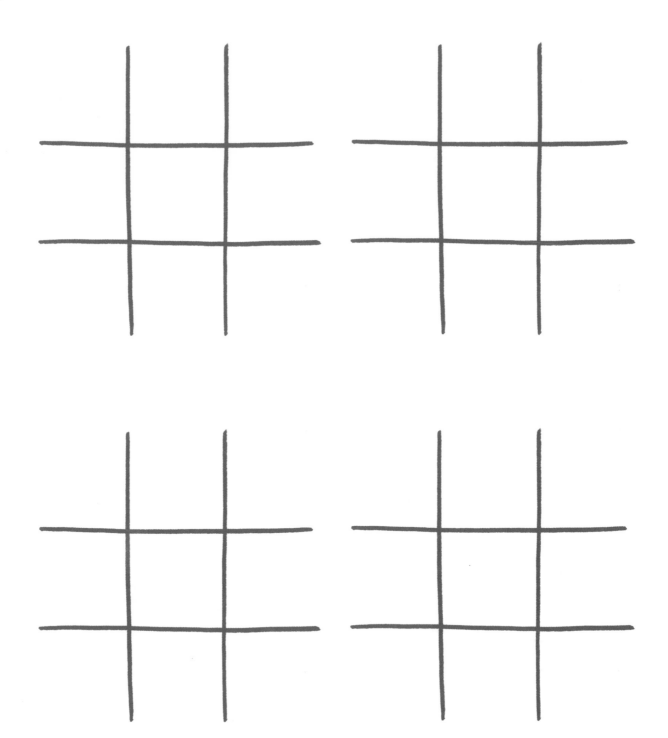

X's anD O's

What you will need:

• two players   • two pencils

Directions:

1. In the grid on the following page, put O's in both bottom corner squares and X's in both top corner squares.

2. Player One will be O and can only place O on the grid. Player Two will be X and can only place X on the grid.

3. Player One begins by putting an O in any square next to a square that already has an existing O. Next, Player Two does the same with an X. Players may only place X's and O's in squares that touch—horizontally or vertically—squares they've already claimed. Players keep filling the grid in this manner.

4. If Player One puts an O in a square, and an adjoining horizontal or vertical square has an X in it, the X square now becomes an O square. Likewise, if Player Two fills in a square with an X, and an adjoining square has an O in it, that square will now become X.

5. The winner of the game is the player who captures all the squares entirely or who has the most X's or O's when every square on the board is filled.

6. You can play the game four more times, using the grids on pages 37 and 38.

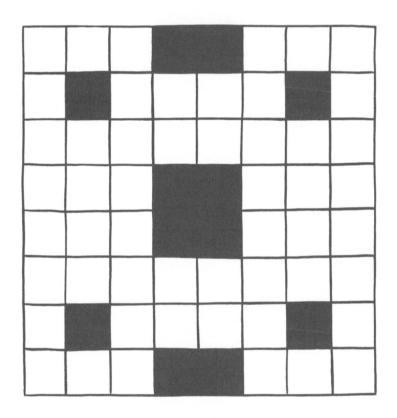

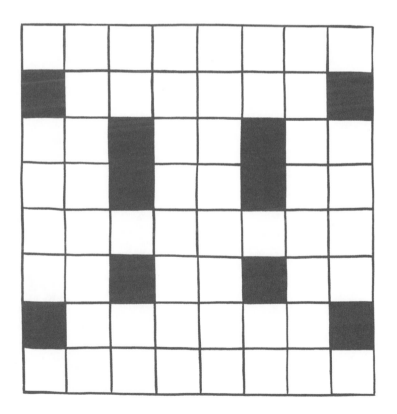

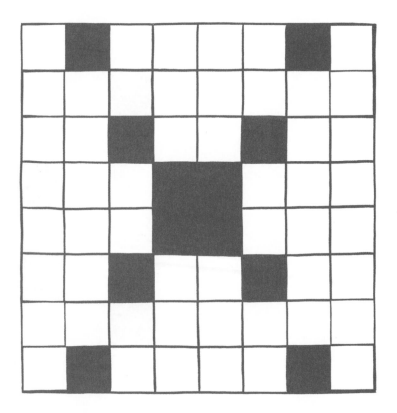

S.O.S.

What you will need:

• two players   • two pencils

Directions:

1. Each player claims a set of grids on the following pages. The grids on the right will be for positioning your own ships, the other for recording your attempts to find your opponent's ships. Make sure you can hide your page from the other player.

2. Each player places four "ships" on the left-hand grid by coloring in three squares in a row, either horizontally or vertically for each ship. Your completed grid will have twelve squares colored in—for four ships.

3. Let the guessing begin! Try to locate your opponent's ships by calling out spots on the grid, like A8 and G5. If you've called out a spot on your opponent's grid that contains a portion of a ship, your opponent must tell you, and, likewise you must tell if your opponent guesses correctly. Mark X's in the boxes in the grid on your right (on pages 40 and 41) that do not contain your opponent's ships. When you do locate a portion of a ship, place a check mark in the box.

4. When your opponent calls out the correct location of a ship on your grid, put a line through that square.

5. The first player to find all the other player's ships wins.

MY SHIPS

	A	B	C	D	E	F	G	H	I	J
1										
2										
3										
4										
5										
6										
7										
8										
9										
10										

MY OPPONENT'S SHIPS

	A	B	C	D	E	F	G	H	I	J
1										
2										
3										
4										
5										
6										
7										
8										
9										
10										

MY OPPONENT'S SHIPS

	A	B	C	D	E	F	G	H	I	J
1										
2										
3										
4										
5										
6										
7										
8										
9										
10										

MY SHIPS

	A	B	C	D	E	F	G	H	I	J
1										
2										
3										
4										
5										
6										
7										
8										
9										
10										

PART TWO

PENCIL PUZZLES

DOODLES: FINISH THE DRAWING

We've started this doodle for you. See how many things you can add to create a wacky scene!

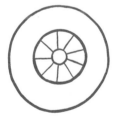 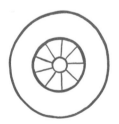

DINOSAUR MAZE

This little dinosaur is trying to find the path that leads back to his friends. Can you help him find it?

(Answer on page 62)

ROCK STAR WORD SEARCH

Draw a line through each word in the puzzle that you see in the list below.
Words appear horizontally, vertically, and diagonally, but always in a straight line.
After you've crossed out the letters used in the puzzle, the remaining letters
form a message for you (and you don't have to unscramble anything!).

L	K	P	S	L	S	B	E	A	T
Y	E	P	A	I	O	B	Y	M	R
R	Y	U	E	O	N	E	A	A	S
I	B	C	I	R	G	G	T	N	I
C	O	D	O	A	F	I	E	S	D
S	A	C	T	N	U	O	S	R	R
R	R	S	Y	G	C	A	R	O	U
U	D	L	O	V	B	E	E	M	M
H	S	T	A	R	E	A	R	R	S
I	N	R	E	C	O	R	D	T	G

band	concert	keyboard	radio	song
bass	drums	lyrics	record	stage
beat	guitar	perform	singer	star

(Answers on page 63)

FOOD ANAGRAMS

Unscramble these delicious words!

naabna	_ _ _ _ _ _	crkscaer	_ _ _ _ _ _ _
cleeyr	_ _ _ _ _ _	yadnc	_ _ _ _ _
ciphs	_ _ _ _ _	pseltzer	_ _ _ _ _ _ _
ockioe	_ _ _ _ _ _	sidcanwh	_ _ _ _ _ _ _ _
daos	_ _ _ _	asott	_ _ _ _ _
dnuhguto	_ _ _ _ _ _ _ _	teolcohac	_ _ _ _ _ _ _ _ _
plape	_ _ _ _ _	beard	_ _ _ _ _
sochan	_ _ _ _ _ _	orpcopn	_ _ _ _ _ _ _
noraeg	_ _ _ _ _ _	akce	_ _ _ _
galbe	_ _ _ _ _	gegs	_ _ _ _
npueats	_ _ _ _ _ _ _	eips	_ _ _ _
secehe	_ _ _ _ _ _	dlsaa	_ _ _ _ _
zapiz	_ _ _ _ _		

(Answers on page 64)

PAPER TELEPHONE

What you will need:

• a few creative friends   • a few pencils

Directions:

1. Tear out this page and flip it over to begin playing. On the other side, you will find a sentence.

2. Draw a picture to illustrate the sentence, then fold the page over at the dotted line so only the picture you drew can be seen. Pass the paper to the next player.

3. The next player writes a sentence about the illustration you drew, then folds the paper at the dotted line so that only the new sentence can be seen by the next player.

4. The next player reads the sentence (not out loud!), then draws an illustration that goes with the sentence, folds over the page at the dotted line, and . . . you get the idea!

5. Do this until there's no more room on the page. Open the paper and read the illustrated story you've all created.

Anna pulled a delicious, hot apple pie out of the oven.

DOODLES: FINISH THE DRAWING

SPOT THE DIFFERENCES

There are ten things that are different between these two pictures. Can you spot all the differences? (Answers on page 62)

WORD LADDERS

You can get from one word to another word by linking them with a word ladder. To do this, start with the given word, then change one letter. Write the new word directly underneath the original, as in the example below. Next, change one letter of the second word, one of the third word, and so on, until you get to the final word on the ladder. Use a pencil with an eraser, in case you make a mistake and want to change your mind.

For example, to get from CAT to DOG by changing only one letter in each word on the ladder, do this:

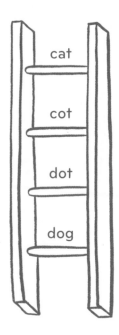

cat

cot

dot

dog

Now you try!
How do you get from
HARD to EASY?

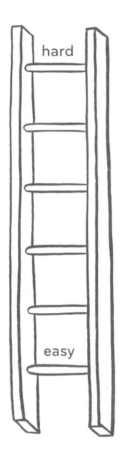

hard

easy

Can you get a
SEED to GROW?

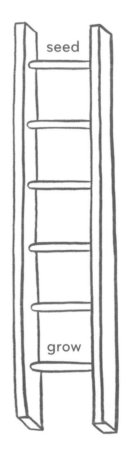

seed

grow

Go from HOME to
TURF. See how many
words it takes!

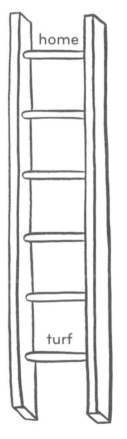

home

turf

(Answers on page 62)

IN THE WILD WORD SEARCH

I	H	W	B	A	N	K	T	R	S
O	M	I	E	U	W	O	A	N	E
E	T	D	P	A	F	U	O	R	A
G	J	E	H	P	G	F	A	O	G
O	I	E	W	A	O	E	A	N	L
R	M	R	J	O	B	E	M	L	E
I	P	U	M	A	L	I	O	N	O
L	R	H	I	N	O	F	O	A	T
L	T	I	G	E	R	T	S	H	E
A	Z	B	I	S	O	N	E	O	O

bear	gorilla	moose
bison	hawk	puma
buffalo	hippo	rhino
deer	jaguar	tiger
eagle	lion	wolf

(Answers on page 63)

SCHOOL DAY anaGRams

Be a good student . . . unscramble these words!

bpacakck	– – – – – – – –	ohtryis	– – – – – – –
achkl	– – – – –	ahtm	– – – –
saeerr	– – – – – –	umcsi	– – – – –
elug	– – – –	senccie	– – – – – – –
rmerka	– – – – – –	coosslarm	– – – – – – – – –
aeprp	– – – – –	edks	– – – –
spne	– – – –	mhkowoer	– – – – – – – –
lerur	– – – – –	iabrlry	– – – – – – –
sisoscrs	– – – – – – – –	nuchl	– – – – –
mcpuorste	– – – – – – – – –	pincipral	– – – – – – – – –
nlegshi	– – – – – – –	ssrcee	– – – – – –
lspncie	– – – – – – –	cheerta	– – – – – – –
ymg	– – –		

(Answers on page 64)

JOIN THE TEAM WORD SEARCH

T	R	A	C	K	C	H	E	S	S
Y	C	O	G	O	L	F	S	O	F
H	S	Y	U	A	S	D	A	F	O
P	O	R	C	I	E	I	I	T	O
O	C	C	N	L	G	V	L	B	T
L	C	N	K	N	I	I	I	A	B
O	E	A	I	E	W	N	N	L	A
T	R	I	I	N	Y	G	G	L	L
N	K	B	A	S	E	B	A	L	L
S	E	R	B	O	W	L	I	N	G

baseball   cycling   golf   sailing   softball

bowling   diving   hockey   skiing   tennis

chess   football   polo   soccer   track

(Answers on page 63)

PAPER TELEPHONE

Jack's dog ran up the tall tree in his backyard.

Make up your own beginning sentence!

UNDER THE SEA ANAGRAMS

Dive right in and unscramble these words!

arbc	— — — —	apdled	— — — — — —
rhsak	— — — — —	siqdu	— — — — —
lacor	— — — — —	bslubeb	— — — — — — —
plindoh	— — — — — — —	ewvsa	— — — — —
toospuc	— — — — — — —	sphmir	— — — — — —
waedese	— — — — — — —	gleogsg	— — — — — — —
tawre	— — — — —	sfhi	— — — —
fplisrpe	— — — — — — — —	adsn	— — — —
ewahl	— — — — —	hlsle	— — — — —
norlkes	— — — — — — —	efre	— — — —
ivde	— — — —	rcenth	— — — — — —
tboa	— — — —	sauberimn	— — — — — — — — —
ssiuwmit	— — — — — — — —		

(Answers on page 64)

SPOT THE DIFFERENCES

There are ten things that are different between these two pictures. Can you spot all the differences? (Answers on page 62)

answers

DINOSAUR MAZE (Puzzle on page 44)

WORD LADDERS (Puzzles on pages 52–53)

HARD	CARD	CART	CAST	EAST	EASY
SEED	SLED	SLEW	SLOW	GLOW	GROW
HOME	SOME	SORE	SURE	SURF	TURF

SPOT THE DIFFERENCES

(Puzzle on pages 50–51)   (Puzzle on pages 60–61)